SPARKLEHORN'S MAGICAL FEELINGS

By Elizabeth Mills

SPARKLEHORN'S MAGICAL FEELINGS

Copyright © 2022 By Elizabeth Mills

Illustrated by Olivier Chen

This Book Belongs to

_____

In a land of myth and magic, where flowers bloom all year, and the air smells sweet like sugar, there lived a little unicorn named Sparklehorn.

Sparklehorn had a special magical power. She had a lot of big feelings and was good at showing them off.

Whenever Sparklehorn felt something BIG, she turned a different color and something magical happened. Sometimes, she wasn't able to handle these big feelings very well.

Sparklehorns's mommy was a wizard with a big mushroom hat. Mommy helped her work through her big feelings that she called emotions, but Sparklehorn needed to learn how to handle those big feelings on her own too!

Sometimes Mommy had to go to work, her job as a wizard was important and she had to leave every evening to help people with her magic spells and potions.

Sparklehorn was proud of Mommy for working so hard. She loved her Mommy very much! So she thought it was never much fun without her home.

When Mommy was leaving, Sparklehorn's fur turned blue. Her wings and mane turned cold and icy, tears gathered in her eyes and she began to cry. Sparklehorn didn't want Mommy to leave. Mommy waved her magic wizard wand and made a stuffed bear appear.

Then she said to Sparklehorn, "You feel SAD when tears fall out of your eyes, and that's important. I miss you when I am at work too! I will be back to kiss you goodnight and read you a story. I will give you a big hug before I go, and when you are sad, you can hug your little bear."

Sad is important. Sparklehorn feels blue because she misses her mommy.

The feeling will
pass eventually,

but until it does,
she can hug her
stuffed bear.
This made her
feel better.

As Mommy was leaving for work, Sparklehorn had a new babysitter arrive at her home. Sparklehorn didn't know what to do and her fur turned a shade of grey. It felt like fish were swimming in her belly because she did not know this new person. She felt SHY.

Sparklehorn hid behind Mommy. Mommy knew just what to say: "I've met the babysitter before, her name is Blossom and I trust her. I would never let someone I don't know watch you while I am at work."

Blossom looked at Sparklehorn and said, "I am so excited to play with you. I know you may feel SHY now, or that it may feel strange meeting new friends at first. But once you get to know me, you may not feel so SHY anymore!"

Sparklehorn still wasn't so sure about Blossom, but once she got to know her, it helped her make a new friend and not feel so SHY.

Blossom pulled out her bag, and Sparklehorn's eyes grew wide. Blossom brought a bag full of brand new toys to play with!

This made Sparklehorn feel very EXCITED and her fur turned yellow and twinkled, sparkling starlight radiated from her wings and formed all around her.

She wanted to prance around the room! Jump up and down!

Sparklehorn felt so EXCITED! She shouted, "Look AT ALL THESE NEAT TOYS!"

Blossom told Sparklehorn, "I'm so glad you like them! When you feel EXCITED you can tell someone and others may be excited too!"

Sparklehorn and Blossom played
with blocks, dolls, and trains.

Sparklehorn felt EXCITED, so she told Blossom, "I am so EXCITED to be able to play with new toys!"

While Sparklehorn was playing with
a new doll, it's head popped off!

This made Sparklehorn's fur turn red. Her mane and wings became firey hot. She was very MAD. Sparklehorn began to scream as flames danced all around her and threw the doll at her babysitter!

Sparklehorn knew this wasn't fair because it wasn't Blossom's fault the doll broke, but Sparklehorn was so MAD. Blossom took a deep breath and told Sparklehorn to take one too. Sparklehorn breathed in through her nose and out through her mouth.

Then Sparklehorn asked for a break
so she could sit by herself for a while
and waited until she was calm.

Sparklehorn was MAD, but she realized that the doll breaking was not a big deal! So as soon as she was calm, she went back to the babysitter and used her words. Blossom was able to fix the doll, and they began to play again.

Everything became alright...

Night came over the land, and stars gleamed in the sky like little bright lights. This made Sparklehorn know that it was time to lie down in bed and Mommy would be home soon. As she was lying in bed, she noticed how dark it was in her room and began to turn purple; this magical feeling made bubbles appear around her and she jumped every time one popped. She felt SCARED. So she grabbed the teddy bear that mommy gave her before she went to work. She started hugging it really tight.

When Sparklehorn hugged her teddy, she stopped feeling SCARED and started feeling braver. There was no reason to be afraid of the dark! Suddenly, she heard someone outside of her door. Sparklehorn hugged her teddy bear tight again. She closed her eyes, and when she opened them she saw...

Seeing Mommy made Sparklehorn very HAPPY. Her fur turned green as she created beautiful flower pedals that swirled around her with the enchanting colors that look like an outdoor garden, it was when she was happy she realized how magical she truly is, and she gave Mommy a big hug!

Mommy told Sparklehorn that when she felt happy she could ask for a big hug and tell someone how she was feeling. She looked at Mommy and shouted "I'm so happy you are home!"

Mommy read Sparklehorn a story, and because they were so HAPPY, they smiled and laughed until it was time to go to sleep.

Sparklehorn felt a lot of big feelings throughout her day. With a little practice and some help, Sparklehorn could figure out which one of her magical emotions she was feeling and knew just what to do when she felt the way she did.

Soon she would realize that her emotions are magical
because feeling things makes her who she is...

... and she is Sparklehorn the unicorn.

CPSIA information can be obtained
at www.ICGtesting.com
Printed in the USA
BVHW061830280822
645472BV00001B/4